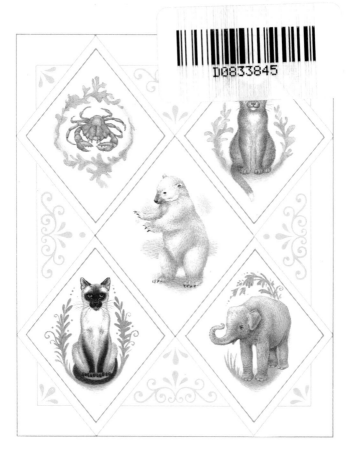
D0833845

For Martina Scrase-Dickins

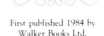

First published 1984 by
Walker Books Ltd,
17-19 Hanway House,
Hanway Place, London W1P 9DL

© 1984 Nicola Bayley

First printed 1984
Printed and bound by
L.E.G.O., Vicenza, Italy

British Library Cataloguing in Publication Data
Bayley, Nicola
Polar bear cat. – (Copycats)
I. Title II. Series
823'.914[J] PZ7

ISBN 0-7445-0153-9

POLAR BEAR CAT

Nicola Bayley

If I were a polar bear
instead of a cat,

I would slide
on my tummy
down hills of snow,

I would be
coloured snow-white,

I would leap
across every gap
in the ice,

I would watch
the beautiful sky
at night,

I would feast
for hours on
freshly-caught fish,

and if ever
I became
too cold or wet,

I would quickly
turn back into
a cat again.